WITHDRAWN

TO GLOUCESTER

M. T. Anderson   illustrated by Bagram Ibatoulline

CANDLEWICK PRESS
CAMBRIDGE, MASSACHUSETTS

IT WAS ON A DAY when the sun was bright,

When the limpets were thick on the rocks,

When the seagulls would squawk

And would talk and would fight

For the fish laid to dry on the docks.

It was on a day when we washed all our clothes,

When we hung them to dry on the frame

Of a little rowboat that would soon be mine.

It was on that day that the serpent came —

It came from the sea, from the lonely sea,

It came from the glittering sea.

I looked down the shore at the water's edge

While hanging my smock out to dry,

And saw, past the ridge of the rocky, old ledge,

Where the moss met the stones and the sky,

The shimmer of ripples, the whip of a tail,

The loops of a beast from the deep.

My mother drew breath and looked paler than death.

I dropped all my socks in a heap.

Then it sank in the sea, in the sunny sea,

It sank in the summertime sea.

I ran to the town, to Gloucester town;

I yelled, "Get your spyglasses out!

We just saw a serpent! We watched it sink down!"

I sped to the dockside to shout.

I sped to the dockside to shout my big news.

They told me to get on inside.

"Yes, we've seen the beast; we beg you, at least,

Climb under something and hide

From that thing in the sea, in the dangerous sea,

In the wide and the terrible sea!"

The terrified townspeople asked, "Is it there?"

They asked, "Has the beast gone away?"

I looked down the lane, past the island where

The schooners lay out in the bay.

The serpent was twirling, just chasing its tail,

And showed all intention of staying.

"Is it back in the deep?" "Is it eating our sheep?"

"I think," I said, "that the serpent is playing.

It plays in the sea, in the frothy sea,

It plays in the wobbling sea."

It played there all day while we watched it from boats.

It played there the next day in rain.

It looked like a line of slippery floats

That swam and that sunk in the main.

It slithered and slid in the bay for a week

And haunted the islands and coves.

And people surprised it asleep on the shore.

And they went out to watch it in droves

As it swam in the sea, in the lovely sea,

As it swam in that ancient, old sea.

In distant cities and towns they soon heard

Of our beast and its tail and its maw.

Zoologists living in Boston sent word

That they wished us to write what we saw.

They wished us to write what we saw, they said.

We saw it by day and by night.

We stood on the dunes as it danced in the moon

And it swam, black-skinned, in the silver light,

As it danced and writhed in the lonely sea,

As it danced in the wide, frosted sea.

When it left, we were sorry and sulked.

We sat on the piers and the docks.

As the haddock were caught and the boats were caulked,

We looked for the beast from our widow's walks.

But the autumn came first, and the winter came next,

And the serpent was not to be seen.

"Oh, it will be back," my mother said,

"When the eelgrass is once again green.

Oh, it will be back, my love, from the sea,

It will be back from the icy, cold sea."

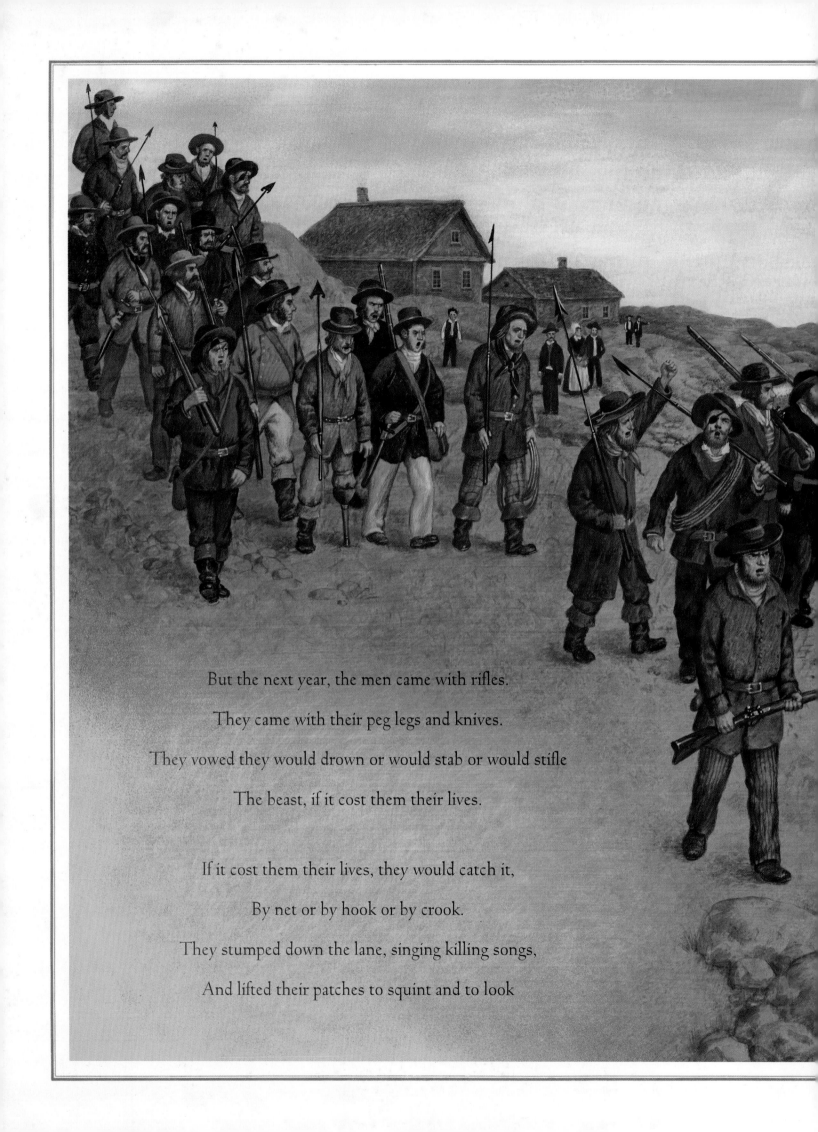

But the next year, the men came with rifles.

They came with their peg legs and knives.

They vowed they would drown or would stab or would stifle

The beast, if it cost them their lives.

If it cost them their lives, they would catch it,

By net or by hook or by crook.

They stumped down the lane, singing killing songs,

And lifted their patches to squint and to look

Far out to the sea, to the lonely sea,

To the murky and murderous sea.

At the murky and murderous sea they stared,

And they hunted its waters in ships.

And their hooks and harpoons were glinting and bare

With sinister, dazzling tips.

They hunted the sea for the serpent.

I rowed in the wake of their whaler.

And I whispered, "Beast, sink. Stay down in the drink."

But I heard the cry of a sailor —

"There! On the sea! On the lovely sea!

I spy the beast on the bounteous sea!"

He pointed his finger; they grabbed their harpoons;

They cast off to chase it in boats.

They rowed to the rhythm of squid-killing tunes

With their bait in their boots and their coats.

They rowed and they crowed and they hollered.

They swore, and they threw their sharp spears.

I saw the red spray and I turned away.

But still I could hear their huzzahs and cheers,

Where they sat on the sea, on the dismal sea,

Near the blood on the wide, dismal sea.

It pulled them left and it pulled them right.

It pulled them up and down.

It tugged them through day and it hauled them through night.

And they feared they would lose it, or drown.

But at last, it gave up its struggle.

They reeled in the rope with their hands.

With grins did they gloat, as they grounded their boat

And they laid their catch, their fresh catch on the sand,

By the side of the sea, the ebbing sea,

By the side of the gray, vacant sea.

It was not a serpent, they saw with a start.

Nothing had gone as they'd wished.

They turned their backs with a heavy heart.

They had landed a pretty big fish.

"I thought surely," protested the captain,

"We brought it to bay on the strand."

But there, with its fins and its grimacing grin

A mackerel lay limp on the land,

Pulled out of the sea, the shifty sea,
The shifty and tricky salt sea.

The sailors, their faces gone gray and weary,

Rowed out to their ships, well defeated.

We waited while mariners, frowning and teary,

Unfurled sails, and halyards were cleated.

And when they had gone, and their sails were small,

I rowed with the fishermen far

Past Loblolly Cove and Norman's Woe

To the place where the sea serpents are.

And we watched them play in that lonely sea,

They twirled in the thundering sea.

IT HAS BEEN MANY YEARS since I was a child,

And I cannot see well or sing.

So I sit by the stove when the storms are wild

And I think of childhood things.

The steamships now plow through the waters.

The forests have been felled by men.

It has been years since the serpent appeared,

And I fear it will not come again, my love,

Though I hope you shall see it,

I fear it is gone —

And I fear it shall not come again, my love,

From the ancient and wrinkled old sea, my love,

From the ancient and wrinkled old sea.

Author's Note ❧

This book is based on a true story. In August 1817, a sea serpent was seen repeatedly around the shores of Cape Ann, in Massachusetts. For days, it played in the harbor. At first, the people of Gloucester were frightened by it, but as time went on, they rowed quite close to it, and several fired on it. It swam under their boats. Col. T. H. Perkins, who traveled to Gloucester to see the monster, wrote, "All the town was, as you may suppose, on the alert; and almost every individual, both great and small, had been gratified, at a greater or lesser distance, with a sight of him [the monster]." After a few weeks, the serpent, or whatever it might have been, disappeared. It was last seen swimming south.

The next summer, it came back. By this point, bounty hunters were trying to capture or kill it. On August 20, 1818, a certain Captain Rich and his crew managed to chase the serpent and harpoon it, but it shook the harpoon loose. They thought they had succeeded again on September 6—but when they finally pulled their catch in, they discovered that what they had landed was a large horse mackerel.

Inhabitants of Cape Ann and the surrounding shores have been describing serpents in their waters since long before the Europeans invaded America. The sightings in 1817 and 1818 were unusual only because so many people saw the monster. Serpents were seen almost yearly throughout the nineteenth century off the New England coast. The sightings petered out in the early twentieth century. Some argue that this is because the serpents followed shoals of fish down the coast every year. When these shoals were fished out, the serpents may have changed their routes or died. Others argue that there never were sea serpents. They suggest that perhaps what people were seeing really was a horse mackerel, like the one Captain Rich caught, or floating seaweed.

Thousands of eyewitness reports of sea serpents, real or imagined, survive. To write this book, I read handwritten accounts of the Gloucester sea serpent sightings that Gloucester resident C. L. Sargent preserved in a little arithmetic notebook, and the publication of a group of amateur zoologists called the Boston Linnæan Society about the Gloucester sightings. A large number of books have been written on the subject of sea serpents; you can read them and decide whether you believe that a serpent ever came to Gloucester. Richard Ellis's *Monsters of the Sea* (Knopf, 1994) is a good introduction to both unknown animals like the sea serpent, and better-known ones like the giant squid. Bernard Heuvelmans's *In the Wake of the Sea-Serpents* (Hill and Wang, 1968) is the most influential and important book on the topic, although it is more than a little eccentric. J. P. O'Neill's *The Great New England Sea Serpent* (Down East Books, 1999) is very complete and responsible in its discussion. For a few more details on Captain Rich's serpent hunt, it's also worth looking at the Cape Ann chapter in R. T. Gould's *The Case for the Sea-Serpent* (Philip Allan, 1930). Perhaps you can be the one to solve the riddle of the serpent so often seen around Massachusetts Bay.

To Mary and John, who live by the sea

M. T. A.

To Martin Straupe, the Greatest Fisherman

B. I.

First edition 2005

Library of Congress Cataloging-in Publication Data

Anderson, M. T.
The serpent came to Gloucester / M. T. Anderson ; illustrated by Bagram Ibatoulline. — 1st ed.
p. cm.
Summary: Rhyming text tells of a sea serpent that plays off the coast of Massachusetts in the summer of 1817,
and is hunted upon its return the next year. Includes a page of facts upon which the story is based.
ISBN 0-7636-2038-6
[1. Sea monsters — Fiction. 2. Fishers — Fiction. 3. Gloucester (Mass.) — History — 19th century — Fiction.
4. Stories in rhyme.] I. Ibatoulline, Bagram, ill. II. Title.
PZ8.3.A5478Se 2005
[Fic] — dc22   2004057921

2 4 6 8 10 9 7 5 3 1

Printed in China

This book was typeset in Truesdell and Carlisle.
The illustrations were done in acrylic gouache.

Candlewick Press
2067 Massachusetts Avenue
Cambridge, Massachusetts 02140

visit us at www.candlewick.com